Copyright © 1999 by Nord-Süd Verlag AG, Gossau Zürich, Switzerland
First published in Switzerland under the title *Cinderella das Aschenputtel*
English translation copyright © 1999 by North-South Books Inc.

All rights reserved.
No part of this book may be reproduced or utilized in any form
or by any means, electronic or mechanical, including photocopying,
recording, or any information storage and retrieval system,
without permission in writing from the publisher.

First published in the United States, Great Britain, Canada,
Australia, and New Zealand in 1999 by North-South Books,
an imprint of Nord-Süd Verlag AG, Gossau Zürich, Switzerland.

Distributed in the United States by North-South Books Inc., New York.

Library of Congress Cataloging-in-Publication Data is available.
A CIP catalogue record for this book is available from The British Library.

ISBN 0-7358-1051-6 (trade binding)
1 3 5 7 9 TB 10 8 6 4 2
ISBN 0-7358-1052-4 (library binding)
1 3 5 7 9 LB 10 8 6 4 2

Printed in Belgium

For more information about our books, and the authors and artists
who create them, visit our web site: http://www.northsouth.com

A FAIRY TALE BY CHARLES PERRAULT

CINDERELLA

ILLUSTRATED BY LOEK KOOPMANS

TRANSLATED BY ANTHEA BELL

NORTH-SOUTH BOOKS · NEW YORK · LONDON

ONCE UPON A TIME there was a nobleman who married again after his first wife had died. His new bride was very haughty, and she had two daughters exactly like herself. The nobleman also had a daughter of his own, the best, sweetest girl in the world, just like her mother, who had been very kindhearted.

As soon as the wedding was over, the girl's stepmother showed her wicked nature. She could not bear to see how good and beautiful her stepdaughter was, for it made her own daughters seem even nastier.

The girl had to do all the unpleasant tasks about the house, scrubbing and sweeping and keeping her stepsisters' beautiful rooms clean and neat, while she herself slept on a wretched straw mattress in a little attic.

The poor girl bore it all meekly and didn't dare tell her father, who would not have believed her, for he was totally under his wife's control. When her work was done, she would lie down by the ashes of the kitchen fire to get a little warmth. So everyone called her Cinderella.

It happened one day that the king's son was to give a ball, and he invited all the nobility of the land, including Cinderella's two stepsisters.

Now there was even more work for Cinderella to do. She had to keep washing and ironing, bringing her stepsisters different dresses and shoes, then putting them away again, and brushing their hair in new ways. She did all she could to make them look beautiful, but even in her ragged clothes she was a thousand times prettier than her stepsisters.

At last the great day came, and the sisters drove off to the ball. Sadly Cinderella watched them go, and she began to weep bitterly.

Now, Cinderella's godmother was a fairy, and she saw all this. "Do you want to go to the ball too?" she asked Cinderella.

"Oh, yes!" sighed Cinderella. "I would love to go!"

"Very well, then," said her godmother. "Go into the garden and fetch me a pumpkin."

Cinderella went into the garden, picked the best pumpkin she could find, and brought it back.

Her fairy godmother touched it with a magic wand and it turned into a coach made of pure gold.

Then the fairy turned six mice into a wonderful team of six beautiful white horses.

But they still needed a coachman, so the fairy touched a rat with her magic wand, and there stood a stout coachman wearing a very fine hat.

Next the fairy said, "Go into the garden and bring me the six lizards you will find behind the well!" And no sooner had Cinderella brought them than her fairy godmother turned them into six footmen.

"There!" Cinderella's fairy godmother told her. "Now you can go to the ball."

"Oh," said Cinderella, "but how can I go to the ball in these old rags?"

Then the fairy touched Cinderella herself with her magic wand, and there she stood in a dress of golden cloth covered with jewels. She wore glass slippers on her feet, the loveliest slippers ever seen.

Cinderella kissed her fairy godmother and climbed into the coach.

"Mind you don't stay after midnight," said the fairy,
"or your coach will turn straight back into a pumpkin,
your coachman into a rat, your horses into mice, your
footmen into lizards, and your beautiful dress will be
nothing but rags again."

Cinderella promised to do as her fairy godmother
said, and she drove happily away.

When she came to the palace, the servants told the king's son that a noble princess had arrived, but no one knew who she was. He hurried to meet her, gave her his hand, and led her into the great ballroom.

The whole room suddenly fell silent. The dancing couples stood still, the violins stopped playing. Everyone gazed at Cinderella's radiant beauty, and then a whisper went around the ballroom. "Heavens above, how lovely she is!"

The king's son himself led Cinderella into the dance, and she danced so prettily that the guests admired her even more.

As for the prince, he had eyes for no one and nothing else. Even when the most delicious dishes were served for supper, he could not eat a morsel.

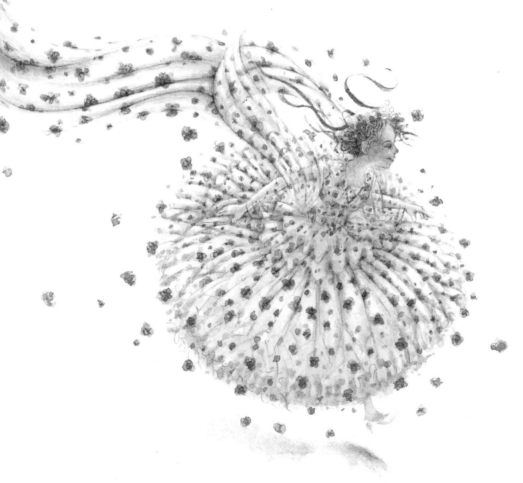

Then, suddenly, Cinderella heard the clock strike a quarter to twelve. She curtsied quickly to the prince and hurried away. No one could stop her.

No sooner was Cinderella home than her dress turned back into rags again.

When her stepsisters got up at noon the next day, they found Cinderella cleaning the floor as usual. They told her how much they had enjoyed the ball, and all about the handsome prince, the wonderful music, and the beautiful unknown princess.

"Did nobody know her at all?" asked Cinderella.

"No, no one knew who she was. She disappeared at midnight, and she wasn't seen again."

Cinderella just smiled and went on washing the floor. Her stepsisters told her there was to be another ball that very evening, and they were both going.

So of course Cinderella went to the ball too. This time her fairy godmother gave her an even more beautiful dress, and rich jewels. The king's son did not move from her side all evening, and said a thousand kind and loving things to her, so that Cinderella quite forgot her promise to her fairy godmother.

When she heard the first stroke of midnight chime, however, she suddenly remembered. She tore herself away from the prince and ran off as fast as a deer.

At first the prince was rooted to the spot. Then he ran after Cinderella. He could not find her, but he did see one of her glass slippers, which she had lost as she ran. Tenderly he picked it up.

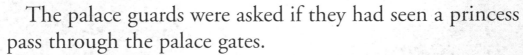

The palace guards were asked if they had seen a princess
pass through the palace gates.

"No, we saw no one," they said. "At least, certainly not
a princess. All we saw was a peasant girl dressed in rags."

Cinderella came home on foot and out of breath, without her coach or footmen. She had nothing left but one glass slipper.

Her two stepsisters told her how the beautiful unknown princess had disappeared again on the stroke of midnight. But she had lost a slipper, they added, and the prince had done nothing at all for the rest of the night but gaze at it. He seemed to have fallen head over heels in love with the mysterious princess.

A few days later the prince announced that he meant to marry the girl whose foot would fit the glass slipper. First all the princesses in the country tried it on, and then the countesses, and then all the other ladies of the court, but it was too small for any of them.

At last the slipper was brought to Cinderella's house, and her stepsisters tried it on, but it did not fit them, either.

"May I try?" asked Cinderella.

At that her sisters laughed mockingly, but the nobleman who was taking the slipper around the town looked closely at Cinderella, and thought she was very beautiful.

"By all means," he said with a smile.

The sisters stared in amazement when they saw that the slipper fitted Cinderella perfectly.

They were even more astonished when Cinderella took the other slipper out of her pocket and put it on, and when her fairy godmother arrived at that very moment and turned her rags into the most beautiful dress ever seen, they recognized her as the unknown princess.

They begged Cinderella to forgive them for all the harm they had done her, and she forgave them with all her heart.

Then Cinderella was taken to the prince, and a few days later they were married.